1 84121 862 6

1 84121 870 7

1 84121 884 7

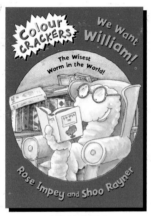

1 84121 876 6

1 84121 868 5

1 84121 886 3

1 84121 874 X

1 84121 872 3

1 84121 890 1

Welcome Home, Barney

The Loneliest Bat in the World!

Rose Impey
Shoo Rayner

ORCHARD BOOKS

ORCHARD BOOKS
96 Leonard Street, London EC2A 4XD
Orchard Books Australia
32/45-51 Huntley Street, Alexandria, NSW 2015
First published in Great Britain in 1995
This edition published in hardback in 2002
This edition published in paperback in 2003
Text © Rose Impey 1995
Illustrations © Shoo Rayner 2002
The rights of Rose Impey to be identified as the author
and Shoo Rayner as the illustrator of this work
have been asserted by them in accordance with the
Copyright, Designs and Patents Act, 1988.
A CIP catalogue record for this book is
available from the British Library.
ISBN 1 84121 882 0 (hardback)
ISBN 1 84121 258 X (paperback)
1 3 5 7 9 10 8 6 4 2 (hardback)
1 3 5 7 9 10 8 6 4 2 (paperback)
Printed in Hong Kong

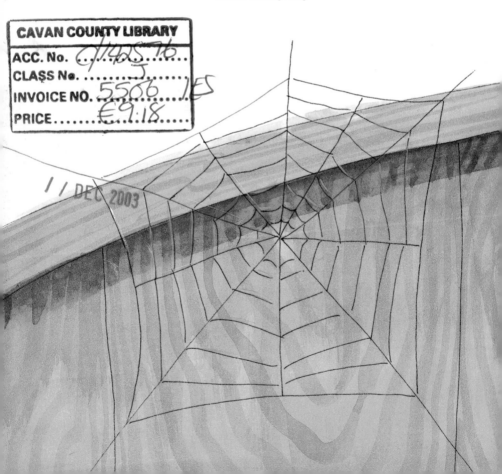

Welcome Home, Barney

Barney the bat lived all on his own.
No mum and dad.
No sisters and brothers.
No mate, to mate with.
Barney was the loneliest bat
in the world.

Barney was lonely
because he was the *only*
large mouse-eared bat left
in the country.
Barney didn't know that.

He thought there must be
other bats, just like him,
somewhere, out there.
He kept hoping he would find one.

Each night, when Barney went out,
searching for food,
he kept one eye open
searching for a mate.

But each night he came home
without one.

Barney had friends, of course,
Owl and Rat and Spider.
"Cheer up," they said.
"You've always got us."
But no matter how hard they tried
they couldn't cheer him up.

"Why don't you take a holiday?"
said Owl.

Travel around.
Visit other places.

So Barney took Owl's advice.

13

Barney travelled all over Britain.
But it didn't suit him.

He got travel sick.
He got homesick.
He got lonely.
Barney came home,
all alone.

"You should pull yourself together,"
said Spider.

Smarten yourself up.
Find a new image.

Barney didn't have *an image.*
He thought he'd better get one.

Barney tried to be cool.

He tried to be punk.

He tried to be sporty.

But nothing seemed to suit him.
He felt silly
and embarrassed
and lonely.
Barney came home,
all alone.

"You're too fussy," said Rat.
"There are lots of other bats
to choose from."

I'll find you a girl.

Barney blushed.
He was very shy.
Even when he found a girl,
he wouldn't know what to say to her.

Rat talked to his friends.

He advertised in the newspaper.

Heartbroken Hedgehog—
prickly outside but soft underneath.
looking for friendship and cuddles.

Mature Mouse—
wants to meet intelligent opera lover.
Two tickets for Die Fleidermouse.

LONELY
Large Mouse-Eared Bat
Seeks
Lady Bat
for
lifetime partnership
serious replies
only
P. O. Box 123

Dashing Dog—
own teeth and hair—
looking for beautiful bitch.
Ring Barking 367

Lonely Owl—
Too sad to give a hoot—
wants flying partner. 28-28-200

He even wrote to Batline.

Rat found lots of girls.
But none of them suited Barney.

Pippi was a pipistrelle bat.
She was too small.

Freda was a fruit bat.
She was a vegetarian.

Err!

Vera was a vampire bat.
She sucked blood!
That didn't suit Barney.

"I'm sorry," he told Rat.
"It's not that I'm fussy.
They're all very nice bats,
but they're not like me."

"Well, never mind," said Rat.
"You've always got your friends."
But it still didn't cheer him up.
Barney hung in the dark
feeling sorry for himself,
all on his own.

It was OK for Owl,
he had a mate.
She had a nest full of baby owls.
Owl had a family.

It was OK for Spider.
She'd made an egg sac
with hundreds of baby spiders in it.
Soon Spider would have
an *enormous* family.

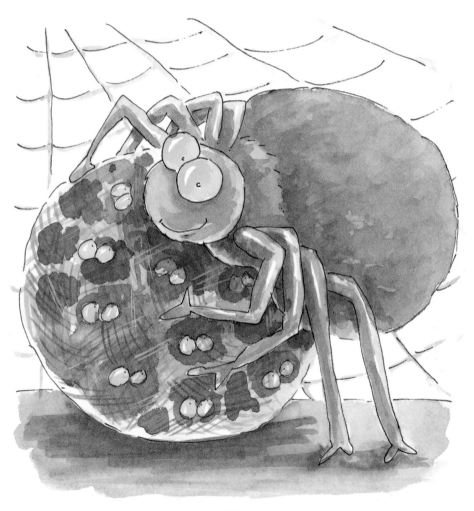

And it was OK for Rat.
Rat had dozens and dozens
of relations.
Rat's family filled the barn.
They were always having
family celebrations.

But Barney had no one –
no one special.
No one to hunt with.
No one to hang out with.
No one to say goodnight to.
Barney was the loneliest
bat in the world.

Then one day Barney woke up.
He was fed up with feeling
sorry for himself.
He decided to do something about it.

Barney hired a private detective,
a mole called Mortimer.

Mortimer sniffed out all the clues
he could find.

"Which do you want first,"
said Mortimer, "the good news
or the bad news?"
"The bad news," said Barney, sadly.
"Well, you're the only one,
I'm afraid. The last of the line."
"The last?" said Barney.

Mortimer nodded.
"You're the last large mouse-eared
bat in the country."
Barney was so disappointed
he started to cry.

"Now, don't get upset," said Mortimer.

The good news is: There are other bats like you, lots of them, all over Europe. You'll have to go abroad, if you want to find them.

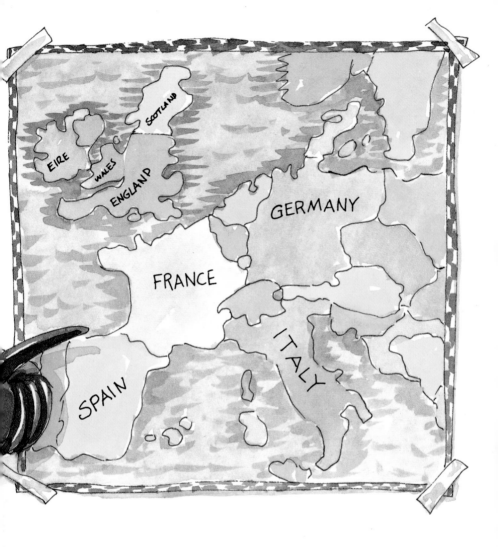

Barney was nervous.
He had never been abroad before.
He might get travel sick.
He might get homesick.
He might get lost.

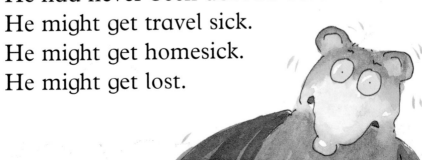

"And we'll all be here,
when you get back," they told him.
That cheered Barney up.

So Barney bought his ticket
and sent for his passport.
He said goodbye to his friends
and flew to France.

When he got there he found
lots of bats like him.
They were very pleased to meet him.

Barney travelled around Germany

and Spain

and Greece.

Wherever he went there were
different places to hunt,
different food to eat,
different bats to meet.

Lots of girl bats, too.
Bella and Bobbie and Bernie.

They each wanted Barney
to stay with them
and settle down,
but he couldn't.

Barney was feeling homesick again.
He had travelled a long way
and found just what he was
looking for.
But all he wanted was to go home.

Barney missed his barn.
He missed the peace and quiet
of his own life.
He missed his friends.

He wondered what they were doing,
back in the barn, without him.

Barney realised for the first time
how much he liked
his life at home.
In the end, Barney knew
he would have to choose.

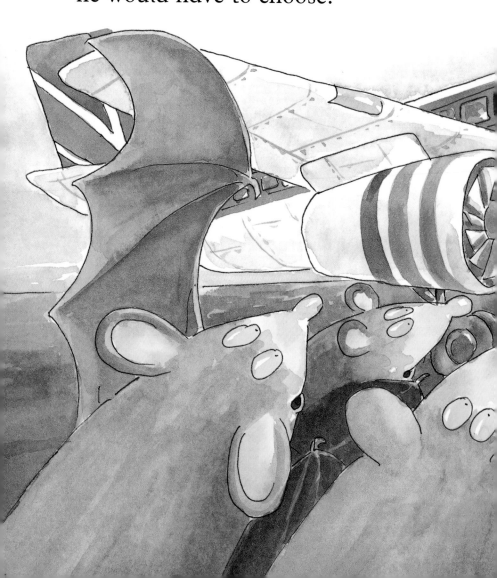

Barney the bat packed his bags,
said goodbye to his new friends
and caught the next plane home.

Barney was pleased to be home.
And his friends were pleased
to see him.
They gave him a Welcome Home party.
"Tell us all about it," said Owl.
"Did you find a girl?" said Rat.
"You look *different*," said Spider.

Barney showed them his photos.
He gave them their presents.
He told them how much
he'd missed them.

"It was a good trip,"
Barney told his new friend, Mortimer.
"But I'm glad to be back.
East or West, home is best.
And home is where your friends are."
"Here's to friendship," said Mortimer.

Crack-A-Joke

Where do vampire
bats keep their money?
In a blood bank!

What fruit do vampire bats like best?
**Blood oranges and
neck-tarines!**

What does a polite vampire say?
Fang you very much!

What is Barney's favourite sport?
Batminton!

Batty jokes to drive you crazy!

Where do you find the most bats in New York?
In the Vampire State Building!

What did the policeman say to the young bat?
Don't let me catch you hanging around here again!

There are 16 Colour Crackers books.
Collect them all!

❏ A Birthday for Bluebell	1 84121 860 X	£7.99
❏ A Fortune for Yo-Yo	1 84121 874 X	£7.99
❏ A Medal for Poppy	1 84121 888 X	£7.99
❏ Hot Dog Harris	1 84121 864 2	£7.99
❏ Long Live Roberto	1 84121 886 3	£7.99
❏ Open Wide, Wilbur	1 84121 884 7	£7.99
❏ Phew, Sidney!	1 84121 872 3	£7.99
❏ Pipe Down, Prudle!	1 84121 880 4	£7.99
❏ Precious Potter	1 84121 868 5	£7.99
❏ Rhode Island Roy	1 84121 878 2	£7.99
❏ Sleepy Sammy	1 84121 870 7	£7.99
❏ Stella's Staying Put	1 84121 890 1	£7.99
❏ Tiny Tim	1 84121 862 6	£7.99
❏ Too Many Babies	1 84121 866 9	£7.99
❏ We Want William!	1 84121 876 6	£7.99
❏ Welcome Home, Barney	1 84121 882 0	£7.99

Colour Crackers are available from all good bookshops,
or can be ordered direct from the publisher:
Orchard Books, PO BOX 29, Douglas IM99 1BQ
Credit card orders please telephone 01624 836000 or fax 01624 837033
or e-mail: bookshop@enterprise.net for details.
To order please quote title, author and ISBN and your full name and address.
Cheques and postal orders should be made payable to 'Bookpost plc'.
Postage and packing is FREE within the UK
(overseas customers should add £1.00 per book).
Prices and availability are subject to change.

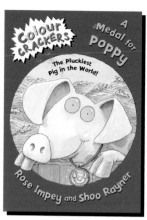

1 84121 888 X

1 84121 862 6

1 84121 870 7

1 84121 878 2

1 84121 876 6

1 84121 868 5

1 84121 860 X

1 84121 874 X

1 84121 872 3